A Surprise in Disguise

Nancy, George, and Bess walked to Mari Cheng's house. There were lots of bushes in front of the house. Their dark green branches were covered with snow.

As the girls got close to the door, Nancy heard a rustling noise in the bushes. "What's that?" she whispered to her friends.

"It's probably just a squirrel," George replied. She reached up to ring the doorbell.

But before she could do that, the rustling noise grew louder. The bushes began to shake, and a puffy cloud of snow rose in the air.

All of a sudden, something jumped out of the bushes toward the girls. It was a weird creature with a tiger face!

"*Grrrr!*" the creature snarled.

The Nancy Drew Notebooks

Available from MINSTREL Books

THE
NANCY DREW
NOTEBOOKS®

#39

The Chinese New Year Mystery

CAROLYN KEENE
ILLUSTRATED BY JAN NAIMO JONES

A MINSTREL® BOOK

Published by POCKET BOOKS
New York   London   Toronto   Sydney   Singapore

The sale of this book without its cover is unauthorized. If you purchased this book without a cover, you should be aware that it was reported to the publisher as "unsold or destroyed." Neither the author nor the publisher has received payment for the sale of this "stripped book."

This book is a work of fiction. Names, characters, places and incidents are products of the author's imagination or are used fictitiously. Any resemblance to actual events or locales or persons living or dead is entirely coincidental.

A MINSTREL PAPERBACK *Original*

A Minstrel Book published by
POCKET BOOKS, a division of Simon & Schuster, Inc.
1230 Avenue of the Americas, New York, NY 10020

Copyright © 2000 by Simon & Schuster, Inc.

All rights reserved, including the right to reproduce this book or portions thereof in any form whatsoever. For information address Pocket Books, 1230 Avenue of the Americas, New York, NY 10020

ISBN: 0-671-78752-7

First Minstrel Books printing December 2000

10 9 8 7 6 5 4 3 2 1

NANCY DREW, THE NANCY DREW NOTEBOOKS, A MINSTREL BOOK and colophon are registered trademarks of Simon & Schuster, Inc.

Cover art by Joanie Schwarz

Printed in the U.S.A.

PHX/[logo]

The Chinese New Year Mystery

1

The Dragon Parade

G*ung Hay Fat Choy!*" eight-year-old Nancy Drew said to her best friend Bess Marvin.

Bess sat down at her desk, which was across the aisle from Nancy's. The two girls were in Mrs. Reynolds's third-grade class at Carl Sandburg Elementary School. The first bell of the day was about to ring.

Bess frowned at Nancy. "*Gung* what?"

"It means 'Wishing you good fortune and happiness' in Chinese," Nancy explained. "That's what people say for Chinese New Year's. Mari taught me."

At that moment Mari Cheng walked into class. She gave Nancy and Bess a little wave.

The school bell jangled noisily. All the students took their seats. Mrs. Reynolds went to the front of the classroom and said, "Good morning, everyone!"

"Good morning, Mrs. Reynolds," the class said all together.

"First I want to tell you about a special art project we'll be doing with Ms. Frick starting tomorrow," Mrs. Reynolds announced. "As you all know, we've been studying Chinese culture for the last month. And this week is the beginning of the Chinese New Year season."

George Fayne raised her hand. George was Bess's cousin and Nancy's other best friend. "But we already had New Year's," George said, looking puzzled. "It was on January first, right? So how can this week be the beginning of the Chinese New Year season?"

"I know!" Orson Wong was waving his arm.

"Yes, Orson?" Mrs. Reynolds said.

"The Chinese New Year is different," Orson said. "It goes on for weeks. We celebrate it at our house. First my mom and dad make us clean the whole house with them. But then we get to eat lots of food, and the kids get red envelopes full of money."

"Thank you, Orson," Mrs. Reynolds said with

a smile. "Orson's right, class. The Chinese New Year season starts about ten days before their New Year's Day, and goes on for a few weeks after that. It's practically a month-long event."

"Cool!" Mike Minelli said, grinning. "Do we get a whole month off from school?"

Mrs. Reynolds shook her head. "Sorry, Mike."

"Too bad," Mike said, making a face.

"The Chinese year is based on the lunar calendar," Mrs. Reynolds went on. She picked up a piece of chalk and wrote the word *lunar* on the blackboard. Next to it she drew a picture of the moon.

"*Lunar* as in moon," she explained, turning to face the class. "Each month of the lunar calendar begins with the new moon. That happens every twenty-nine or thirty days. Not like our months, which can be thirty-one days long. Which means that as far as we're concerned, the Chinese New Year falls on a different day every year. On the other hand, our New Year's Day is always on January 1."

She added, "Also, each new year has a name based on an animal. The year of the Dragon, the year of the Rat . . . there are twelve animals in all."

3

Bess raised her hand. "So what's our special art project, Mrs. Reynolds?"

"Some communities mark the end of the Chinese New Year season with a dragon parade," Mrs. Reynolds replied. "Even if it's *not* the year of the Dragon. For the Chinese, the dragon represents strength and brings good luck. A couple of people wear a big dragon costume. Everyone else follows them with lanterns and banners and masks."

Her eyes twinkling, she added, "Mrs. Apple and I decided that our two third-grade classes will have a dragon parade two weeks from today. Her class will make the lanterns, banners, and masks. Our class will make the dragon."

A dragon! Nancy thought. That seemed like a really cool project. She tried to imagine a dragon so big that more than one person would have to carry it.

All the kids in the class started buzzing excitedly about the dragon parade. Then a loud voice drowned out everyone else's. "Two weeks from today? No way! It has to be on a different day."

Nancy turned around in her seat. The loud voice belonged to Brenda Carlton.

"Brenda, is there a problem?" Mrs. Reynolds asked her.

"I won't be here that Monday," Brenda complained. "My mom and dad are taking me out of school to go to Wisconsin. There's a big party for my grandparents' wedding anniversary." She crossed her arms over her chest and glanced around the classroom. "I'm sure everyone agrees that we can't have the parade without me."

Bess rolled her eyes at Nancy. Brenda always acted like she was the most important person in the whole world.

"Your father spoke to me about that," Mrs. Reynolds told Brenda. "I'm sorry, but the date can't be changed. The parade is going to be in the gym after school, and that Monday is the only day the gym is free."

"But that's totally not fair!" Brenda cried out.

"I know. But I'm sure you'll have fun helping the class make the dragon," Mrs. Reynolds said. "Anyway, you'll all be starting the dragon project tomorrow in Ms. Frick's art class. Right now let's get back to our lesson on Chinese culture."

* * *

Later, during lunch, Nancy sat in the cafeteria with Bess and George. They munched on their sandwiches and talked about the dragon parade.

"I saw a picture of a dragon parade once," George told her friends.

"My parents took me to Chinatown in Chicago last summer," Bess said. "They had the coolest clothes stores there!"

Nancy took a sip of her milk and smiled. Bess was really into clothes and shopping. George wasn't like that at all. She was much more into sports and stuff like that. Sometimes it was hard to tell that the two of them were cousins.

Just then Mari came up to the table where the girls were sitting. Mari smiled shyly at them and said, "Um, do you want to come to my house for dinner tonight? Afterward, we're going to do this special ceremony—the Kitchen God ceremony. It's to start the Chinese New Year season. Anyway, my parents said it would be okay if I invited all of you."

"Sounds great," Bess said eagerly. "I'll just have to ask my parents."

"Me, too," Nancy said.

"Me, three," George chimed in.

"Great. You can come over at five," Mari said.

"I think the Chinese New Year is *stupid*."

Nancy turned around in her chair. Brenda was sitting at the next table with her best friend, Alison Wegman. Alison was in Mrs. Reynolds's class, too. It was Brenda who had spoken.

Mari's brown eyes grew enormous. She looked as though she was about to cry. "I-it's not s-stupid," she said to Brenda in a shaky voice.

"Well, I think it is," Brenda insisted. "Why should I help the class make a dragon when I'm not even going to be here for the parade? I think the whole thing is stupid!"

"Just ignore her," Nancy whispered to Mari. But Mari didn't say anything. She just gave Nancy and her friends a little wave and headed for the cafeteria line.

"Why does Brenda have to be such a baby about everything?" Bess complained.

It was a few minutes before five. She, George, and Nancy were heading up the walk to Mari's house for dinner. They were all looking forward to the special New Year's ceremony.

7

Nancy stuffed her hands into the pockets of her blue parka. The air was cold and crisp. There was still snow on the ground from a storm the week before. The girls' boots made loud crunching noises as they walked.

"Brenda's just mad because she can't be in the parade," Nancy said to her friends.

"She was really mean to Mari," George pointed out.

"I know. She shouldn't have made fun of the Chinese New Year," Nancy said.

The Chengs' house was brick with bright red shutters. In front were lots of bushes. Their dark green branches were covered with snow.

As the girls got close to the door, Nancy heard a rustling noise in the bushes. "What's that?" she whispered to her friends.

"It's probably just a squirrel," George replied. She reached up to ring the doorbell.

But before she could do that, the rustling noise grew louder. The bushes began to shake, and a puffy cloud of snow rose in the air.

All of a sudden, something jumped out of the bushes toward the girls. It was a weird creature with a tiger face!

"*Grrrr!*" the creature snarled.

2

The Kitchen God

Nancy and her friends stared in horror at the tiger creature. It raised its arms in the air. *"Grrr! Roarrrrr!"*

Bess screamed. So did Nancy and George.

Then Nancy realized that the weird creature wasn't a creature at all. It was a person wearing a tiger mask.

"Wh-who are you?" Nancy stammered.

"Vincent! What are you doing?"

Mari was standing at the front door. "What are you doing to my friends?" she said angrily to the boy.

Vincent pulled off the tiger mask. He glanced at Nancy, Bess, and George. Then he laughed in a mean way. "Scared you, didn't I?"

Bess put her hands on her hips. "That wasn't very nice," she told him.

"I'm really sorry about him," Mari said apologetically to Nancy, Bess and George. "This is my cousin, Vincent Li. He's in seventh grade at Dewitt Middle School." Dewitt was a town near River Heights. "He's here for dinner, and so are my aunt Rose and uncle Roger and—"

Mari was interrupted by the sound of someone giggling. The giggling was coming from the bushes.

The bushes started shaking again. Then a little boy of six or so jumped out. His black hair had clumps of snow in it.

"That was cool, Vincent!" he said. "Supercool!"

"Thanks, Shrimp," Vincent said.

"This is Sammy, Vincent's brother," Mari explained to the girls. "Vincent, Sammy . . . these are my friends Nancy, Bess, and George. They're having dinner with us. So please be nice," she finished in a stern voice.

Vincent just smirked and didn't say anything. He scooped up a handful of snow and

11

packed it into a big snowball. He turned to face George with a nasty gleam in his eye.

"Don't you dare!" George yelled.

Vincent laughed and pretended to throw the snowball at her. At the last minute, he threw the snowball at Sammy's feet instead. It exploded into a cloud of snow. Sammy giggled loudly and jumped up and down.

"Come on," Mari said to the girls. She led them into the house. It was warm inside, and the air was filled with wonderful, spicy smells.

"I'm sorry again about Vincent," Mari said as she hung up everyone's parkas. "He's a big bully, and he likes to pick on me. And my friends, too." She added, "Sammy's okay, except that he looks up to Vincent way too much."

"I'm glad I don't have a brother like Vincent," George said. She sniffed at the air. Are we having chicken for dinner?"

"Why do you ask?" Mari said.

"Because you said something about the Chicken God's ceremony," Bess replied.

Mari laughed. "No, not the Chicken God, silly. The *Kitchen* God. Come on, let's see if dinner's ready."

All the grown-ups were in the kitchen. Mari introduced Nancy and her friends to her parents, Mr. and Mrs. Cheng, and to her aunt Rose and uncle Roger, who were Vincent and Sammy's parents.

"We're so glad you could join us," Mr. Cheng said cheerfully to the girls.

"I hope you like Chinese food," Mrs. Cheng added.

Nancy glanced at the kitchen counter. On it were platters heaped with yummy-looking dishes: shrimp, steamed dumplings, stir-fried vegetables. A pot of soup was bubbling on the stove. It smelled like lemon and herbs.

"I *love* Chinese food," Bess said. Nancy and George nodded.

Everyone helped carry the platters to the dining room table. When they sat down to eat, Vincent and Sammy were across from Mari and Nancy. Vincent whispered something in Sammy's ear, and Sammy giggled.

Mrs. Li frowned at her sons. "That's enough, boys. Vincent, please pass the rice."

Nancy picked up the pair of chopsticks next to her plate. They were red with a pretty gold design.

"Red and gold are New Year's colors," Mari

explained. "Red stands for happiness, and gold stands for wealth."

Mari picked up her own chopsticks and showed Nancy how to eat with them. It was hard at first, but then Nancy got the hang of it.

"Look!" Nancy said to Bess and George. She lifted a dumpling with her chopsticks and popped it into her month.

Bess and George tried to do the same with their chopsticks. After a few minutes, they got the hang of it, too.

Mr. Li smiled at Nancy, Bess, and George. "Are you young ladies familiar with the Chinese New Year holiday?"

"We're learning about it in school," Nancy said. "Our teacher said that the New Year season lasts for weeks."

"Yes," Mari said, nodding. She explained how many families celebrated. First they spent several days cleaning their houses in order to "sweep out the old and welcome the new." Then they decorated with scrolls, paintings, flower arrangements, and bowls of fruit.

As Mari spoke, Nancy glanced around the dining room. A beautiful scroll painting of snow-covered flowers hung on the wall. Next to it, on a table, were a vase filled with plum blossoms and a bowl heaped high with shiny orange tangerines.

"Tonight we will be honoring the Kitchen God," Mrs. Cheng said. "In another week it will be New Year's Eve, and then New Year's Day. And even after New Year's Day things still go on . . ."

"Like the dragon parade," Mari said. She told her mother and the others about the dragon parade they would be having at school. She also told them about the dragon they were making.

"It's going to be really cool," Bess said.

"It sounds pretty lame, if you ask me," Vincent mumbled.

"Yeah," Sammy echoed, bouncing up and down in his chair. "Lame!"

"Vincent! Sammy! Apologize to our guests!" Mr. Li scolded them.

"Yeah, whatever, sorry," Vincent muttered.

"Yeah, whatever, sorry," Sammy said, too.

Nancy took a sip of her soup and stared at Vincent. Why was he so mean?

Mr. Li frowned at his sons and then changed the subject. He told everyone that he and his family were thinking of moving to River Heights. The rest of the dinner was spent talking about the different neighborhoods in town.

When everyone was finished eating, Mr. and Mrs. Cheng called everyone into the kitchen.

Mari's parents had set up a plate of cakes and a bowl of tangerines on the counter next to the stove. There was also a stick of incense burning in an incense holder. The smoke gave off a sweet, flowery smell.

On the wall next to the counter was a painting of a man wearing a colorful robe. "That is the Kitchen God," Mr. Cheng explained to Nancy, Bess, and George. "The Kitchen God watches over everything, and we have tried hard to please him by cleaning and decorating our house. Now we are offering him a special dinner of sweet foods. We will then pray for him to go up to the heavens and say good things about our family."

Everyone gathered around the counter. Mr. Cheng said some words in Chinese. After he was done, he took the picture of the Kitchen God from the wall. Then he lit a match and set the picture on fire.

"Why are you doing that?" Bess asked, her eyes wide.

"We are sending him on his way to the heavens so he can report on our family," Mr. Cheng explained.

Later, as Nancy, George, and Bess were getting ready to leave, Mrs. Cheng said, "I'm so glad you girls could join us this evening. Perhaps you can all come back on Saturday night for our New Year's Eve feast."

"Feast? As in more totally yummy Chinese food?" Bess said eagerly. "Count me in!"

Nancy was excited. She couldn't wait for New Year's Eve. Still, she wondered if the Li family would be at the feast, too. She liked Mari's aunt Rose and uncle Roger, but Vincent was definitely no fun to be around!

"To make the dragon, we'll start with the head."

It was Tuesday afternoon. Ms. Frick, the art teacher, was showing Nancy and her classmates how to make the dragon. Ms. Frick was tall and had short, wavy brown hair. She was wearing long, dangling earrings shaped like tulips.

Nancy was sitting with Bess, George, and Mari at one of the big round art tables. In the middle of the table were art supplies: scissors, paint, paintbrushes, glue, and boxes of colorful beads, feathers, and sequins.

Ms. Frick held up some newspapers. She explained how they would cut the newspapers into strips to make the dragon's head out of papier-mâché. Then they would paint the head and decorate it with the beads, feathers, sequins.

"Then we'll attach a couple of bamboo sticks to the base of the head," Ms. Frick explained. "Two people will carry the dragon. Whoever is up front will hold the bamboo sticks."

George raised her hand. "How will we make the dragon's body?"

"We'll sew pieces of red silk together and attach them to the head," Ms. Frick replied. "It will be like a long, flowing robe, and we can decorate that, too." She added, "The person who carries the dragon in the back will have the silk part draped over his or her head."

Brenda pretended to yawn. "This is *soooo* boring."

"There goes Miss Snooty Pants again," George whispered to Nancy.

The class got started on the dragon's head. Nancy loved papier-mâché. It was fun slapping the wet, slimy, gloopy pieces of newspaper together and making a shape out of them.

Nancy couldn't wait for the dragon parade. The night before, Mrs. Cheng had said that she would lend Nancy, George, and Bess some red silk Chinese outfits to wear.

That's going to be so awesome, Nancy thought.

After a while, the dragon's head was done. It just needed to dry. Nancy thought the dragon's head looked really big and scary, even though it didn't have eyes or a nose or mouth yet.

Just then Mrs. Reynolds walked into the room. She had a small paper bag in her hands.

"I have all your names in here on little pieces of paper," she announced to the class. "I need to pick two students to carry the dragon during the parade."

Orson Wong raised his hand. "Pick me, Mrs. Reynolds!"

"I have to pick the names at random, Orson," Mrs. Reynolds told him. She reached into the bag and plucked out two pieces of paper. "George Fayne and Alison Wegman," she read.

"Cool!" George said.

"Definitely," Alison agreed. Then she glanced over at Brenda and said quickly, "I mean, it won't be much fun without *you*, Brenda."

Nancy peered over at Orson. He was frowning. Nancy figured that he was mad about not being picked.

Ms. Frick looked up at the clock. "Let's start cleaning up, everyone. Please straighten up your tables. And the dragon head needs to dry. Maybe we should put it in the big supply closet so that it's out of the way."

Orson's hand shot up in the air again. "I'll do it, Ms. Frick."

"Okay, Orson." Ms. Frick pointed to the head, which was resting on one of the tables. "Please be careful with it, okay? Do you want some help?"

"No, I can do it myself," Orson replied. He picked up the head gingerly, so he wouldn't get his fingers too gooey with papier-mâché paste. Then he started toward the closet.

But before he had taken even two steps, he tripped.

"Oops!" he cried. The dragon head flew out of his arms and into the air. It hit the floor with a terrible splat.

3

Dra-gone!

Nancy gasped as she watched the dragon head hit the floor. Was it totally ruined?

Orson fell, too. "Ow, my knee!" he complained.

Ms. Frick and Mrs. Reynolds rushed up to him. "Are you okay, Orson?" Mrs. Reynolds asked him.

Orson rubbed his knee. "I guess so. I might need a bandage, though. Maybe one of those cool purple ones."

Nancy went over to the dragon head. She turned it over carefully. It was a little dented on one side. But the rest of it seemed okay.

"Is Mr. Dragonhead totally destroyed?" Orson said to Nancy. "Too bad!"

"It's just dented a little," Nancy told Orson. But she wondered about Orson's weird statement. It was almost as though he'd *wanted* the dragon head to be totally destroyed.

Ms. Frick picked up the dragon head and studied it. "Nancy's right. We can fix it, no problem."

The class went back to cleaning up. While everyone was busy, Nancy tried to figure out what Orson had tripped on. She couldn't find anything on the floor.

Had he really tripped by accident? Nancy wondered. Or had he done it on purpose? He had seemed pretty mad that Mrs. Reynolds hadn't picked his name out of the bag. Could he have been mad enough to try to ruin the dragon head?

"Let's give him ears, okay?" George said to Nancy, Bess, and Mari.

It was recess on Friday. The four girls were in the playground, making a snowman.

Mari scooped up a handful of snow and started shaping an ear. "This is almost as much fun as making the dragon," she said cheerfully.

Nancy made an ear, too, and pressed it against the snowman's head. "I wonder if we'll finish the dragon today," she said to her friends.

They had been working on the dragon for the last three days in Ms. Frick's art class. First they'd repaired the head. Then they'd made the body out of silky red fabric.

Yesterday they'd sewed and glued decorations onto the dragon's head and body: feathers, beads, and sequins. Now all that was left was to give the dragon eyes and a nose and a mouth. Ms. Frick had said that they could put some gold tassels on the dragon, too. At the very end, they would attach two bamboo sticks to the dragon head with a special kind of heavy tape and more papier-mâché.

"Hmm. We should give this snowman a cool outfit or something," Bess said thoughtfully.

Nancy giggled. "Or maybe— Hey!"

A snowball smacked Nancy on the shoulder. "Who did that?" she cried out, brushing at her parka.

Then she saw. On the other side of the schoolyard fence was Vincent, Mari's cousin.

Behind Vincent, Mari's aunt Rose and uncle Roger got out of a car, followed by Sammy.

Vincent smiled at his parents innocently. "Here we are at Carl *Sandbug* Elementary School," he announced.

"Sandbug," Sammy repeated, jumping up and down. "Sandbug, Sandbug, Sandbug!"

"That's enough, boys," Mr. Li told them.

Mari rushed up to the fence. Nancy, George, and Bess ran after her. "Aunt Rose! Uncle Roger! What are you all doing here?" Mari said, looking puzzled.

"The Dewitt schools are having parent-teacher conferences today, so it's a half day," Mrs. Li told her. "Hi, girls. It's nice to see you again."

"We told you the other night that we're thinking about moving to River Heights," Mr. Li said. "We have an appointment to talk to your assistant principal, Ms. Oshida. We want to see how this school would be for Sammy."

"It's a totally great school," Bess said enthusiastically. "The best thing is, you can walk from here to the Double Dip. They have awesome hot chocolate there!"

While everyone else was discussing the school, Nancy turned to Vincent and glared at him. She was angry about the snowball.

But she didn't want to get into a fight with Vincent in front of his parents.

After exchanging goodbyes, the Li family headed into the school. Nancy and the girls played for a while longer until it was time to go in.

As they headed across the playground, they ran into a bunch of girls from Mrs. Apple's third-grade class: Rebecca Ramirez, Lindsay Mitchell, Amara Shane, Jennifer Young, and Laura McCorry. They were heading inside, too.

"We were just talking," Rebecca said, falling into step beside Nancy. "It is *so* not fair that your class gets to make the dragon for the parade. I mean, our class has to make all the boring stuff, like masks and lanterns and banners. But you get to make the big, huge, major centerpiece of the whole parade!"

Rebecca and Nancy often walked to school together. Rebecca wanted to be an actress when she grew up. She always acted as if everything was a big drama.

"Making masks and lanterns and banners sounds like fun," Nancy said with a smile.

Lindsay frowned. "Not as much fun as making the dragon."

"Yeah," Amara agreed.

"Yeah," Jennifer and Laura echoed.

The five girls from Mrs. Apple's class headed over to Ms. Frick's room for their art period. Nancy, Bess, George, and Mari headed for Mrs. Reynolds's classroom.

As they walked, Nancy wondered why Rebecca and the others were acting so weird about the dragon. It wasn't such a big deal that Mrs. Reynolds's class was making the dragon instead of Mrs. Apple's class.

Or was it?

An hour later Nancy and the others in Mrs. Reynolds's class filed into Ms. Frick's room for their art period. Ms. Frick was peering under all the tables with a frown on her face.

"What is it, Ms. Frick? Did you lose something?" Nancy asked her curiously.

Ms. Frick's eyes were troubled. "It's the dragon," she replied. "I got it out so you could all start working on it. Then I left the room for a few minutes—and now it's gone!"

4

A Blue Clue

Nancy gasped. How could the dragon be gone?

She thought quickly. "Where did you leave it, Ms. Frick?" she asked.

The art teacher pointed to one of the tables near the door. "Over there. And then I remembered that Ms. Oshida wanted to talk to me. So I went to her office, spoke with her, and came back."

"How long were you gone?" Nancy asked.

"About ten minutes at the most," Ms. Frick said.

Nancy nodded. "Did you leave the door open?"

"Yes," Ms. Frick said, shrugging. "I didn't think anything of it."

"Nancy's a detective, remember?" Bess reminded Ms. Frick. "She can find the dragon."

"Or not," Brenda muttered under her breath.

Nancy frowned at Brenda. Why was she being even snootier than her usual snooty self?

Nancy and her classmates searched all over the art room for the dragon. They looked under tables, behind chairs, and on the shelves along the wall. But the dragon was nowhere to be found.

Nancy spent a long time at the table near the door where Ms. Frick had left the dragon. The dragon could have been seen from the doorway, she realized. Anyone could have walked down the hall, seen it sitting on the table, and taken it.

But who would have done such a thing? Nancy wondered. And why? And how could the thief have hidden something so big?

Then something caught Nancy's eye. Under the table was a small, round piece of blue cloth. She picked it up.

The piece of cloth was a patch. A red, fire-breathing dragon was stitched on it.

Nancy turned the patch over. There were

loose blue threads on the back and at the edge. It looked as though it might have fallen off a person's jacket or something.

George came up to her. "Did you find something, Nancy?" she whispered.

"A clue," Nancy whispered back excitedly.

Just then Mrs. Reynolds popped her head in the doorway. Ms. Frick rushed up to her and told her what had happened.

Mrs. Reynolds's expression grew serious. "Did anyone in here have anything to do with this?" she said after a moment.

No one said a word. Nancy noticed that Orson was staring really hard at the floor. Brenda had a smug-looking smile on her face.

Mrs. Reynolds and Ms. Frick had a quick, whispered conversation. Then Mrs. Reynolds turned to the class.

"The dragon didn't walk off by itself," she said slowly. "Until it's returned, it might be best if we postponed the parade. After all, the dragon *is* the most important part of the parade."

"You've got to find the dragon, Nancy!" Mari said.

It was Saturday night, the eve of the Chinese New Year. Nancy, Bess, George, and Mari were hanging out in Mari's room. Her parents were preparing the New Year's Eve feast in the kitchen. The house smelled really wonderful.

Nancy knew that Mari's uncle Roger and aunt Rose were in the kitchen helping out. Some other relatives would be coming later. Vincent and Sammy were in the basement playing video games.

Nancy was sitting on Mari's bed with her special blue notebook propped against her knees. Her father had given her the blue notebook to help her solve mysteries. She liked to write down clues and suspects whenever she was working on a case.

"If we're going to find the dragon, we have to come up with some suspects," Nancy said to her friends.

"I think Brenda did it," George said right away.

"Yeah. Brenda was acting all snooty because she couldn't be here for the dragon parade," Bess reminded everyone. "Maybe she took the dragon so we couldn't have the parade."

Mari turned to Nancy. "What do you think? Do you think Brenda's the thief?"

"Maybe," Nancy replied. She picked up her pen and wrote:

SUSPECTS
Brenda Carlton

Nancy stopped writing for a second. "What about Orson? Remember when he tripped the other day and the dragon's head got dented? I couldn't tell if he did that on purpose or not."

"Why would Orson take the dragon?" George asked her.

"Orson seemed kind of mad when Mrs. Reynolds didn't pick his name out of the bag," Nancy explained. "Maybe he wanted the parade canceled, too."

"Yeah," Bess agreed. George and Mari nodded.

Nancy picked up her pen again and wrote "Orson Wong."

Then something else occurred to her. "What about Rebecca and all those girls from Mrs. Apple's class?" she said. "They were acting really weird about the dragon yesterday at recess."

34

"They had their art period before ours yesterday," George pointed out.

"I'll add them to the suspect list," Nancy said, scribbling. "But I'm still not sure how the thief—"

"Or thieves," Bess corrected her.

"Or thieves got the dragon out of the room without someone seeing it," Nancy said.

A few minutes later, Mrs. Cheng called the girls into the dining room for dinner. The other relatives had arrived: more aunts and uncles and cousins. Nancy counted twenty chairs at the dining room table.

Nancy glanced at the array of food. There was a steaming bowl of soup at each place setting. In the middle of the table were platters of fried noodles, whole fish and lobsters, roast chickens, and ribs with barbecue sauce. Every-thing looked so yummy!

Vincent was standing at the end of the table. He smiled when he saw Nancy and the girls.

"Hi, how are you all doing this fine evening?" he said in a polite, friendly voice.

Nancy frowned. Why was he being so nice all of a sudden?

Vincent pulled a chair out for each of the

girls. "Here, allow me to help you," he said.

"Um, thanks," Nancy said, sitting down. Bess, George, and Mari did the same. Bess gave Nancy a look: What's up with him?

After everyone was seated and introductions were made, Nancy picked up her special Chinese spoon. The soup looked really delicious. It had pieces of shrimp and scallops in it, and vegetables, and . . .

Suddenly Bess screamed.

"There's something in my soup!" she cried. "And it's alive!"

5

The Super-Duper-Secret
Project

Get that thing out of my soup!" Bess yelled.
She jumped up from her seat. Her chair fell
backward with a loud thump.

"What is it, Bess? What's in your soup?"
Nancy cried.

Bess pointed to her soup. "Th-th-that," she
said in a shaky voice.

Nancy leaned over and peered into Bess's
bowl. She saw shrimp, and scallops, and vegetables and . . .

. . . a slimy brown worm!

Sammy started giggling. Nancy glanced at
him and then at Vincent. Vincent was staring
at his plate. He was trying to hide a smile.

"What is going on? What is wrong with my soup?" Mrs. Cheng said in alarm.

Nancy looked down at her own soup. There was a worm in it, too.

She picked up a wooden chopstick and dipped it into her soup. She draped the worm over it.

"Oh, gross!" George exclaimed.

Nancy peered closely at the worm. "It's fake," she announced. She peered at George's and Mari's bowls. There were fake worms in them, too.

Sammy giggled even harder. Vincent started laughing, too.

That explains why Vincent was so nice to us a few minutes ago, Nancy thought. He wanted me, Bess, George, and Mari to sit in the seats with the wormy soup bowls.

"You guys did this, didn't you?" Nancy said to Vincent and Sammy.

Mr. Li put down his spoon. "Apologize to our guests," he said to his sons in a stern voice. "Immediately! Or no *hongbao* for you."

"*Hongbao?*" Nancy whispered to Mari. "What's that?"

"Red envelopes with good luck money," Mari whispered back. "The grown-ups give

hongbao to the children on New Year's Eve."

"So-rry," Vincent said to the girls in a mock-serious voice.

"Sammy!" Mrs. Li prompted him.

Sammy banged his feet against the rungs of his chair. "So-rry," he said, in the same tone of voice as his brother.

Mrs. Cheng got Nancy, Bess, George, and Mari fresh bowls of soup. Everyone picked up their spoons and chopsticks and began eating again. Vincent and Sammy didn't try to pull any more tricks the rest of the meal.

Later that night Nancy was at home, getting ready to go to bed. Her dog, Chocolate Chip, was already asleep. She was curled up on the floor next to Nancy's bed. Her tail made soft little thumping noises.

Nancy put on her pajamas with the tiny pink roses. She got out her blue detective's notebook and opened it to the page about the missing dragon. She lay down on her bed and started reading what she had written.

There was a knock on the door. "Come in!" she said.

The door opened a crack. Her father poked his head in. "Hi, Pudding Pie. I came to say good night."

Carson Drew walked in. He was tall and handsome, with brown hair and a warm smile. "Pudding Pie" was his special name for Nancy.

Mr. Drew sat down at the edge of her bed and kissed her on the head. "Solving a mystery?" he asked. He was a lawyer, and he often helped Nancy with her cases.

"Yes, Daddy," Nancy replied. "I'm solving a very important mystery." She told him all about the missing dragon. She explained that Mrs. Reynolds was postponing the parade until the dragon was found.

Mr. Drew looked thoughtful. "Hmm. Do you have any suspects yet?"

"Brenda Carlton, Orson Wong, and a bunch of girls from Mrs. Apple's class," Nancy said. "You know, Rebecca, Lindsay, Amara . . . those girls."

Mr. Drew nodded. "Uh-huh. And what about motives?"

"They all have motives," Nancy said, sitting up a little. "Brenda's motive is, she's mad because she can't be at the dragon parade.

Orson's mad because he didn't get picked to be one of the dragon carriers. And Rebecca and those girls are mad because our class gets to make the dragon."

"What about clues?" Carson asked her.

Nancy showed her father the blue dragon patch that she'd found in Ms. Frick's room. "I think maybe it fell off of someone's jacket," she said. "I'm not sure if it was the thief's jacket, though."

Carson Drew turned the patch over in his hands. "Looks like a pretty good clue to me," he said after a moment. "Have you tried to find its owner yet?"

Nancy shook her head. "Not yet."

"I think that should be your next step, Pudding Pie," Carson said, ruffling her hair.

"Gung Hay Fat Choy!" George greeted Nancy and Bess.

The three girls were walking down the street. It was a bright, cold day out. Sunlight sparkled on the snow-covered ground.

It was Sunday, Chinese New Year's Day. Mari was at home with her family. She had explained to the girls that on New Year's Day it was traditional to stay at home and receive guests all day long.

"*Gung Hay Fat Choy!*" Nancy said back to George. "Okay, where to first? Brenda's house?"

"Sure, let's go see Miss Snooty Pants," Bess said cheerfully.

After talking to her father the night before, Nancy had formed a plan. She, Bess, and George would show the blue dragon patch to each of their suspects to try to figure out who the owner was.

They soon reached Brenda's house. Brenda herself answered the door.

"What do you want?" Brenda said. She crossed her arms over her chest. She didn't look very happy to see them.

"Can we come in? It's freezing out here," Nancy said.

"Oh, I guess," Brenda said with a dramatic sigh. She opened the door a little wider. Nancy, Bess, and George stomped the snow from their boots and walked into the front hall.

"Okay, so what do you want?" Brenda demanded.

Nancy reached into her pocket and pulled

out the blue dragon patch. "You dropped this in the hallway the other day," she fibbed. "I've been meaning to give it to you."

Brenda peered at the dragon patch. "That ugly thing is totally not mine," she said. "As usual, you three don't know what you're talking about."

Bess's hands flew to her hips. "That is a mean thing to say, Brenda Carlton!" she exclaimed. "But you're just a mean person, aren't you? You were mean enough to steal the dragon just because you couldn't be in the dragon parade, and—"

"Bess!" Nancy and George said at the same time.

A nasty smile spread across Brenda's face. "Is that why you're here?" she said. "Because you think I stole that stupid old dragon? You're crazy!"

Nancy turned to Brenda. "Well, did you?"

"No!" Brenda said. "If I wanted to mess up your stupid old dragon parade, I would have thought of a better way."

"Like what?" George asked her.

"Like, why would I tell you?" Brenda retorted. "Now, if you don't mind, I have important things to do."

The girls went to Orson Wong's house next. He was at home, along with his parents and his twin six-year-old brothers, Lonny and Lenny. Other people were there as well, visiting the family for New Year's Day.

Lonny and Lenny were marching around the living room, banging on toy drums and singing at the top of their lungs. People drifted in and out of the kitchen with cups of tea and plates of sweets. Music was playing on the CD player.

"Can we talk to you somewhere quiet?" Nancy asked Orson.

"Sure. Follow me to my Chamber of Horrors," Orson said.

Orson led the three girls to his room. Nancy and her friends had been in it before. There was a big blue globe on his dresser and bug mobile hanging from the ceiling. Orson's desk was covered with rocks and minerals and plastic dinosaurs. Nancy didn't see anything horrible, except for Orson's pet iguana. It was sitting very still in its cage and staring at the girls with its big, bulging eyes.

Then Nancy noticed something weird next to the iguana's cage. It was big and lumpy-

45

looking. She couldn't tell what it was exactly because it was covered with a white sheet.

"What's that?" she asked Orson.

"Oh, that. That's my super-duper-secret sculpture project," Orson said mysteriously.

"Oh," Nancy said. She pulled the blue dragon patch out of her jeans pocket. "Is this yours? We found it in the hallway."

Orson grabbed the patch from her and studied it. His eyes gleamed. "No. But it's cool. I think I'll keep it." He started to stuff it into his pocket.

As he was doing that, something fluttered out of his pocket. Nancy reached down to pick it up.

It was a small piece of red silk. It was the same color silk that they'd used to make the dragon.

"*You* stole the dragon!" Nancy said to Orson.

6

Lost and Found?

Nancy waved the piece of red silk at Orson. "You're the dragon thief!" she accused him.

Orson blushed. "I d-did not steal the d-dragon!" he stammered. "No way!"

"Then where did you get this red silk?" George demanded suspiciously.

"Yeah," Bess said, frowning.

"Yeah," Nancy echoed.

Orson looked down at the ground, then at the ceiling, and then, finally, at the girls. "Oh, okay," he mumbled. "I did steal the silk. I mean, I kind of borrowed it. But I didn't steal the dragon!" he insisted.

"What do you mean you borrowed it?" Nancy asked him.

Orson sneaked a quick glance at his super-duper-secret sculpture project. Nancy wondered why.

I guess there's only way to find out, she thought.

She walked over to Orson's super-duper-secret sculpture project. She yanked the sheet off it.

"Hey!" Orson protested.

Underneath the sheet was a big cardboard box with a little cardboard box stuck on top of it. It looked kind of like a robot. All kinds of things were glued onto it: pieces of construction paper, buttons, beads, feathers, sequins . . .

. . . and scraps of red silk!

"I—I can explain," Orson said nervously. He handed the patch back to Nancy. "I found the silk and some of this other stuff in Ms. Frick's trash can the other day. I figured I could bring it home since it was garbage. I wanted to use it for Metalor the Mutant."

Nancy was confused. "Metalor the Mutant?"

Orson pointed to the robot. "That's his

name. Metalor the Mutant. My super-duper-secret sculpture project."

Nancy stared at the robot. It seemed as if Orson was telling the truth. The trash can in Ms. Frick's classroom, which was really big, was always full of scraps and stuff.

Then another thought occurred to Nancy. Orson could have taken the things out of Ms. Frick's trash can and stolen the dragon, too.

But how can I find out? Nancy wondered.

"There's nothing like hot chocolate with whipped cream to help you solve a mystery," Bess said.

She dipped her spoon into her mug and swirled it around. Then she raised the spoon to her lips and licked all the whipped cream off it.

She, Nancy, and George were at the Double Dip. It was their favorite place to get ice cream in the summer and hot chocolate in the winter.

Nancy had her special blue notebook out, opened to the page about the missing dragon.

She took a sip of her hot chocolate and said, "We still have to talk to our other suspects."

"Who's that?" George asked her.

Nancy tapped her pen against the notebook. "The girls in Mrs. Apple's class, remember? Rebecca, Lindsay, Amara, Jennifer, and Laura."

"You mean, we have to go to all their houses? Like now?" Bess sighed. "In that case I'm going to need another cup of hot chocolate. You know, for the energy."

George peered over Nancy's shoulder. "I don't think you're going to be needing that extra hot chocolate, Bess. Guess who just walked into the Double Dip?"

Nancy turned around. Rebecca and Amara were coming through the front door. They were laughing about something. The two girls sat down at a table on the other side of the room.

"I'm going over to talk to them," Nancy announced to her friends. "Stay here, okay?"

Nancy got up and walked across the room. Rebecca and Amara had their heads bent close. They were drinking hot chocolate, too, and talking in low voices.

Nancy caught the words "the dragon." Rebecca was saying something about the dragon, she realized. But before she could

51

hear any more, Rebecca looked up sharply.

"Nancy Drew! You're eavesdropping!" Rebecca said in an accusing tone of voice.

Nancy stopped in her tracks. "No, I'm not. I just came over to say hi," she said.

"You were eavesdropping," Rebecca insisted.

Nancy pulled the blue dragon patch out of her pocket. "Actually, I wanted to ask you guys about something. Does this belong to either of you?"

"No," Amara said, shaking her head. Rebecca shook her head, too.

Nancy stuffed the patch back in her pocket. "Okay. Thanks. Just wondering." She smiled at the girls and walked back to her table.

"Well?" Bess said eagerly as Nancy sat back down.

Nancy leaned forward and lowered her voice. "I'm not totally sure. But I think that Rebecca and the other girls might know something about the missing dragon."

Nancy, Bess, and George waited until Rebecca and Amara had left the Double Dip. Then they quickly paid their check and followed the two girls.

"Why are we doing this again?" George whispered to Nancy as they walked down the street. They hung back thirty or forty feet behind Rebecca and Amara. "I feel like a spy or something."

"It's just a hunch," Nancy whispered back. "Rebecca and Amara might lead us to the dragon."

Rebecca and Amara ended up at Rebecca's house and went inside. Nancy, Bess, and George walked quietly up to Rebecca's bedroom window.

Nancy and her friends stood on their tippy toes and peered into the window. It was frosted over with ice, so it was a little bit hard to see inside.

Rebecca and Amara were sitting on Rebecca's bed. They were looking at something that was on the bed, and talking.

Nancy rubbed at the frosty windowpane with her mitten. She squinted to get a better look. Then she gasped.

Lying on the bed was the missing dragon!

7

Rebels and Dragons

Nancy couldn't believe it. The dragon was right there on Rebecca's bed!

"What's going on?" Bess whispered.

Nancy moved aside to let the cousins take a look. She pointed to the dragon. "See?" she whispered excitedly.

"Ohmigosh!" George exclaimed. Then she clamped her hand over her mouth. "I mean, ohmigosh," she whispered.

Nancy started for the front door. "Come on."

Nancy rang the bell. After a moment, Mrs. Ramirez answered it. She had a cup of tea in one hand and a magazine under one arm.

"Oh, hello, girls," she said cheerfully. "Come on in. Rebecca's in her room."

"Yes, we know," Bess said.

Mrs. Ramirez looked confused. George jabbed Bess with her elbow.

"I mean, we figured she might be," Bess said quickly.

Nancy, Bess, and George headed down the hall to Rebecca's room. The door was closed. Nancy didn't want to knock to let Rebecca and Amara know they were there. She thought they might try to hide the dragon.

Nancy took a deep breath. Then she opened the door and burst into Rebecca's room. "Surprise!" she yelled.

Bess and George followed behind her. "Dragon thieves!" George said angrily to Rebecca and Amara.

Rebecca and Amara jumped up from the bed. They looked really shocked. "Huh? What are you talking about?" Rebecca demanded.

"That," Nancy said, pointing to the dragon. Then she did a double take. She walked over to the bed to take a closer look. What she was looking at wasn't the stolen dragon, after all. It was just a big heap of red silk. The fabric was draped over a couple of pil-

lows. Through Rebecca's frosty window, the big red heap had looked like the dragon.

"I guess . . . uh . . . oh, well, I'm sorry," Nancy stammered. She felt really bad about making a mistake.

"You should be," Amara said huffily.

"I don't get it, though," Nancy said, confused. "Why were you guys talking about the dragon at the Double Dip?"

"So you *were* eavesdropping!" Rebecca accused her.

"Well, yes, kind of. I'm sorry about that, too," Nancy apologized.

Rebecca and Amara exchanged a glance. Then Rebecca sat down on the bed.

"Okay, this is the story," she began. "We were really, really super-mad that your class got to make the dragon for the parade. It was so unfair! But then Amara came up with this awesome idea."

"We'd make our own dragon," Amara piped up eagerly. "Then we'd surprise everyone with it at the parade. Two dragons are better than one, right?"

"We figured Mrs. Reynolds and Mrs. Apple wouldn't say no if we just showed up with it," Rebecca added. "They'd see how much work we put into making dragon number two."

"Except now there's not going to be a parade," Bess pointed out. "I mean, it's been postponed until dragon number one is found."

Rebecca shrugged. "I know. That's why we kind of put Project Dragon Number Two on hold." She added, "Amara and I were just trying to figure out what to do with all this red fabric."

"Where did you get it?" George asked.

"My mom was going to make a dress out of it a long time ago," Amara replied. "I asked her if I could have it, and she said yes."

Nancy's mind was racing. Rebecca and Amara and the other girls from Mrs. Apple's class were no longer suspects. That left Brenda and Orson.

But she couldn't prove that the dragon patch belonged to Brenda *or* Orson. And they had both denied stealing the dragon.

Now what? Nancy wondered.

Nancy's gaze fell upon Rebecca's desk. It was really, really messy with piles and piles of stuff.

Just then Nancy noticed something. On top

of one of the piles was a copy of Brenda's newspaper, the *Carlton News*. On the front cover was Brenda's usual gossip column.

It's probably full of snooty rumors, Nancy thought.

There was also a story about the new, low-fat ice cream being served in the cafeteria. The headline read: "Low-Fat or Low-Taste? You Decide!"

Finally, there was a story about the middle-school basketball championship. The headline read: "River Heights Rebels Totally Rule Over Dewitt Dragons in City Championship!"

Rebels and Dragons, Nancy thought.

Then it came to her. She grinned at her friends. "Rebels and Dragons!" she said out loud.

Bess frowned at her. "Huh? What are you talking about, Nan?"

"Is that a new rock group or something?" Amara asked her. "That's kind of a dumb name."

"I think I know who stole our dragon," Nancy announced, her eyes sparkling.

"What!" Rebecca exclaimed. "You must tell us immediately!"

Nancy held up the copy of Brenda's paper and pointed to the headline about the Rebels and Dragons.

"I found a blue dragon patch in Ms. Frick's room," Nancy told Rebecca and Amara. "We were thinking that it might have dropped off someone's jacket."

"Someone as in, the dragon thief," George piped up.

Nancy nodded. "Right. Well, what if the dragon patch belonged to a Dewitt Dragon? Who do we know that goes to Dewitt Middle School?"

Bess gasped. "You mean . . ."

"Exactly," Nancy said excitedly. "Mari's cousin Vincent!"

8

Gung Hay Fat Choy!

Nancy was sure of it. Vincent was the dragon thief.

"Vincent!" George said, her eyes wide. "But how could he have stolen the dragon?"

"Remember? The Lis were at our school on Friday," Nancy reminded her. "Vincent must have gone off on his own and found the art room somehow. I guess he sneaked in there while Ms. Frick was away and took the dragon."

"That makes total sense to me," Bess said. "Vincent would do something like that. Remember how he scared us with that tiger mask? And how he put those yucky, disgusting, gross-out worms in our soup?"

"We were talking about the dragon parade on the night of the Kitchen God ceremony," George remembered. "So Vincent knew how important the dragon was to us."

"Wow!" Amara said in amazement. "Mystery solved. Okay, so now what?"

"So now we have to find Vincent and make him confess," Nancy said.

"I think Mari said that all the Li family was at their house today for New Year's," George said.

Nancy stood up. "Let's go!"

Nancy, George, and Bess rushed over to Mari's house. Mari answered the door. "Hi, what's up?" she said to Nancy and the girls.

"Can we come in?" Nancy asked her.

Mari nodded and opened the door wider. Then she led Nancy and the others into the living room.

The scene at the Chengs' house was a lot like the scene at Orson Wong's. Dozens of relatives were milling around the living room, drinking tea and eating sweets. There were lively conversations going on both in Chinese and in English.

On the coffee table was a big tray full of

62

different kinds of food. Mari told the girls that the tray was called a *Chuen-Hop*—the "Tray of Togetherness." She pointed out the different foods. "That's candied lotus seeds there . . . and candied melon . . . and coconut," she explained.

"Mari, where's Vincent?" Nancy asked in a low voice.

"I think he and Sammy are in the basement," Mari replied. "Why?"

Nancy told Mari about her theory about Vincent. Mari looked shocked.

"You think *Vincent* did it?" Mari said.

Nancy nodded. "I do. But we have to talk to him first."

Mari's brown eyes were blazing. "Okay. Follow me."

Nancy grabbed some lotus seeds from the Tray of Togetherness and popped them into her mouth. They were delicious. Then she followed Mari and the others down the hall and down a flight of carpeted stairs.

In the basement, Vincent and Sammy were at the Ping-Pong table. Vincent seemed to be teaching Sammy how to play.

"Okay, Shrimp," Vincent was saying, gesturing with his paddle. "The point of the game is to slam the ball as hard as you can. Hit your opponent if you can. Oh, and here's a really good way to cheat, especially if you're way behind . . ."

Nancy cleared her throat, and Vincent glanced up.

"Hey, ladies! Want to play Ping-Pong with us?" he said cheerfully.

"Oh, yeah, right," Bess said, rolling her eyes.

Nancy pulled the blue dragon patch out of her pocket. "Is this yours, Vincent?"

Vincent took the patch from her and studied it. "Yeah, I guess. Actually, I noticed that it was missing from my jacket a couple of weeks ago. Why?"

"A couple of weeks?" Nancy was confused. She had found it in Ms. Frick's room on Friday, which was just two days ago.

There must be an explanation, she thought. Or maybe Vincent was lying. Out loud, she said, "Okay, Vincent, just admit it. You stole the dragon, didn't you?"

"Dragon? What dragon?" Now Vincent looked confused.

"The dragon we were making for the New Year's parade," Mari spoke up. "How could you steal it, Vincent? You knew how important it was to all of us!"

"I didn't steal it," Vincent insisted. "But I wish I had," he added with a sly grin. "What a totally awesome prank!"

Nancy heard someone giggling. She turned around.

Sammy had his Ping-Pong paddle over his mouth. But the paddle didn't stifle his giggles.

Then it dawned on Nancy.

"Sammy," she said slowly. "Did *you* take the dragon?"

Sammy stopped giggling. He looked down at the floor and nodded.

"Sammy!" Mari cried out.

Vincent stared at his little brother in shock. "You did it, Shrimp?"

Sammy nodded again. "We were at the Sandbug School with Mom and Dad," he explained. "I had to go to the bathroom. I walked past a room and saw the big red dragon on a table."

"And so you just stole it?" George said in amazement.

Sammy shrugged. "No, not really. I was trying to do a funny prank, like Vincent. So I went into the room. Nobody was in there. And I . . ."

"You what?" Mari prompted him.

"I hid it in the, um, garbage can," Sammy replied.

Nancy, George, Bess, and Mari exchanged a glance. "The garbage can!" George cried out. "That means . . . that means . . ."

"That means the dragon might have gotten shredded into a million-billion pieces in some sort of weird compactor thing-y," Bess moaned.

"Or maybe not," Nancy said.

Nancy asked Mari if she could use the phone. She called Ms. Frick at home.

Then Ms. Frick called the janitor.

Then Ms. Frick and the janitor went over to the school together.

An hour later Nancy and the girls heard the whole story. On Friday the janitor had emptied all the trash cans—including the one from the art room—into the main Dumpster. He'd been in a hurry and hadn't noticed the big red dragon in the trash can.

Fortunately, the Dumpster hadn't been emptied yet. Ms. Frick and the janitor managed to find the red dragon in there, safe and sound.

"I can't believe the parade is really happening!" Bess whispered to Nancy.

"This is so exciting!" Nancy whispered back.

The day of the parade had finally arrived. The school gym was a sea of people: students, teachers, and parents.

The kids in Mrs. Reynolds's class were in one corner of the gym. The kids in Mrs. Apple's class were nearby.

Nancy, Bess, George, and Mari were all standing together. They were wearing the special red Chinese outfits that Mrs. Cheng had lent them.

Nancy glanced out at the crowd. Her father was there, and Bess's parents, and George's parents, too. She also saw Mr. and Mrs. Cheng, Mr. And Mrs. Li, and Vincent and Sammy.

Mari followed Nancy's gaze. "Sammy apologized to my aunt and uncle about the dragon," she whispered. "And he apologized to Ms. Frick and Mrs. Reynolds." She added,

"My aunt and uncle talked to Vincent, too. Vincent's been setting a bad example for Sammy."

"What about the dragon patch?" George piped up. "How did that end up in Ms. Frick's class?"

"I guess it fell off Vincent's jacket weeks ago," Mari explained. "Sammy found it and decided to keep it. Then he accidentally dropped it when he was in Ms. Frick's room."

Just then Mrs. Reynolds walked up to George, carrying the red dragon. Alison Wegman came over, too. Nancy thought the dragon looked really awesome with all the feathers, beads, sequins, and gold tassels on it. It had cool-looking black eyes, and a nose and a big mouth painted on it, too.

"Are you ready?" Mrs. Reynolds asked George and Alison.

The two girls took the dragon from her and nodded eagerly. "Ready!"

"We're ready, too," Mrs. Apple called out. Rebecca and Amara held up their dragon.

Lively Chinese music began playing on the P.A. system. Nancy could hear drums and flutes in the music, and a stringed instrument, too.

George put the head of the dragon over hers and held the bamboo sticks firmly with both hands. Alison stood about four feet behind George. She draped the red silk body of the dragon over her head like a cape.

Rebecca and Amara did the same with their dragon. All the other third graders picked up the lanterns, banners, and masks that the kids in Mrs. Apple's class had made. Nancy lifted up a shiny lantern. So did Bess. Mari picked up one of the banners together with Orson Wong.

Mrs. Reynolds gave a signal. George and Alison started forward with their dragon, with the other dragon right behind. All the other kids followed behind the two dragons.

Nancy watched as George and Alison made their dragon sway back and forth with their hands and bodies. It looked as though the dragon was dancing a really wild, crazy dance.

As the music played, the third-graders made their way around the gym in a big, wide circle. The parents and teachers clapped and cheered.

"This is totally cool!" Bess said to Nancy.

Mari fell in step with Nancy and Bess.

"This parade never would have happened without you, Nancy," Mari said with a happy smile.

"I'm just glad we solved the mystery," Nancy said, smiling back. *"Gung Hay Fat Choy!"*

"Gung Hay Fat Choy!" Mari and Bess said in unison.

Later that night, before Nancy went to bed, she got out her special blue notebook and began to write:

The dragon parade was a big success! It was really fun. It's been really fun learning about the Chinese New Year season, too.

There's something else I learned. Little kids like to copy what big kids do. That's okay, unless the big kid is someone mean like Vincent! Maybe Vincent will start being nicer from now on.

Gung Hay Fat Choy! Case closed.